The
STARLIGHT
BABY

For my Sasha Starlight.
∽ G. S.

For my dear children Esme and Samuel.
∽ E. H.

SIMON & SCHUSTER BOOKS FOR YOUNG READERS
An imprint of Simon & Schuster Children's Publishing Division
1230 Avenue of the Americas, New York, New York 10020
Text copyright © 2005 by Gillian Shields
Illustrations copyright © 2005 by Elizabeth Harbour
Originally published in Great Britain in 2005 by Simon & Schuster UK Ltd.
Published by arrangement with Simon & Schuster UK Ltd.
First U.S. edition 2006
All rights reserved, including the right of reproduction in whole or in part in any form.
SIMON & SCHUSTER BOOKS FOR YOUNG READERS is a trademark of Simon & Schuster, Inc.
Book design by Genevieve Webster
The text for this book is set in Garamond.
The illustrations for this book are rendered in watercolor.
Manufactured in China
2 4 6 8 10 9 7 5 3 1
CIP data for this book is available from the Library of Congress
ISBN-13: 978-1-4169-1456-3
ISBN-10: 1-4169-1456-0

The
STARLIGHT
BABY

By
GILLIAN SHIELDS
Illustrated by
ELIZABETH HARBOUR

SIMON & SCHUSTER BOOKS FOR YOUNG READERS
New York London Toronto Sydney

There was a baby who had no mother,
crying in the starlight.
And as the stars burned,
the baby's tears called to the watching world.

"Stars, bright stars,
can you love me?
Will you be my mother?"

But the stars shone fiercely, far away in the deep sky.

"Moon, silver moon,
can you warm me?
Will you be my mother?"

But the moon blinked cold and pale above the world.

"Wind, west wind,
can you hear me?
Will you be my mother?"

But the wind grew wild and howled over the hills.

"Trees, oh trees,
will your branches hold me?
Will you be my mother?"

But the trees shook their heads in the hurrying wind.

"Hill, gray hill,
will you shelter me?
Will you be my mother?"

But the hill slept on, crouching over its stony heart.

"Wolf, wild wolf,
can you feed me?
Will you be my mother?"

But the wolf licked her cubs and snarled in the shadows.

"Stream, clear stream,
will you wash me?
Will you be my mother?"

But the stream rushed over its bright bed and could not stop.

There was a woman who did not smile,
because she had no child.

She sat at her window,
looking up at the stars,
and the wind carried the cry of a baby to her heart.

"Can you hear me?
Will you feed me, warm me, hold me, wash me, shelter me?
Can you love me?"

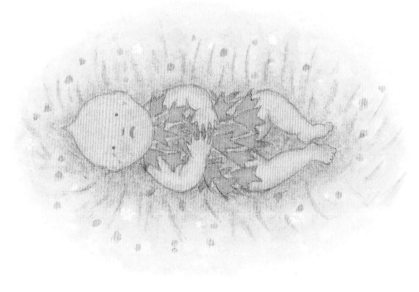

And the woman answered,

"Yes."

She ran out into the night and the moon lit her path.

The stream led her down the hill.

The trees swayed in the wild wind to point the way.

The wolf's tracks made a trail for her to follow,
until, at last, she came to the place...

...and found the baby, lying under the stars.

"I will be your mother, little one," she said.

So the baby stopped crying.
And the woman smiled.

Then the night was over, and the morning star shone out,
as they went home together.